DARK HUNTER
SHIP OF DEATH

First US edition published in 2015 by Lerner Pubishing Group.

Text Copyright © Benjamin Hulme-Cross, 2013
Illustrations Copyright © Nelson Evergreen, 2013
This American Edition of *Ship of Death*, First Edition, is published by Lerner
Publishing Group, Inc., by arrangement with
Bloomsbury Publishing Plc.

Cover design: Dan Bramall. Cover photo: Shutterstock.

Main body text set in Times LT Std. 17/22
Typeface provided by Adobe Systems.

Darby Creek
A division of Lerner Publishing Group, Inc.
241 First Avenue North
Minneapolis, MN 55401 USA

For reading levels and more information, look up this title at
www.lernerbooks.com.

Library of Congress Cataloging-in-Publication Data

Hulme-Cross, Benjamin.
    Ship of death / by Benjamin Hulme-Cross ; illustrated by Nelson Evergreen.
  — American edition.
      pages cm. — (Dark Hunter)
    Summary: Mr. Blood, Edgar, and Mary face a ghostly ship that takes them
on the ride of their lives.
    ISBN 978-1-4677-5727-0 (lb : alk. paper) — ISBN 978-1-4677-8090-2 (pb :
alk. paper) — ISBN 978-1-4677-8660-7 (eb pdf)
                                                    tural—Fiction.
                                                    tle.

                                                    2015002295

DARK HUNTER

SHIP OF DEATH

BENJAMIN HULME-CROSS

ILLUSTRATED BY NELSON EVERGREEN

darbycreek
MINNEAPOLIS

The Dark Hunter

Mr. Daniel Blood is the Dark Hunter.
People call him to fight evil demons,
vampires, and ghosts.

Edgar and Mary help Mr. Blood
with his work.

The three hunters need to be strong and
clever to survive . . .

Contents

Chapter 1

The Ship

There was an old, ruined ship in the harbor. Nobody was on deck. Torn sails hung from its masts like dead skin. It looked like a wreck, but it was still floating.

Mr. Blood put his spyglass down.

"How long has the ship been there?" Mary asked Tom, the old harbor master.

"We saw it at dawn two mornings ago," said Tom. "It must have come in during the night."

"And nobody has left the ship or come onshore?" asked Mr. Blood.

"That's right," said Tom. "I've watched it. No one has come up onto the deck."

"Maybe it's just a wreck. Maybe it just drifted into the harbor," said Edgar.

"That can't be right," said Tom. "Look, it has an anchor."

Edgar looked through the spyglass. He could see a chain running down into the water from the front of the boat.

Old Tom was right. Somebody must have let down the anchor.

"And there's something else I have to tell you," said Tom. "This isn't the first time that ship has come here."

"Go on," said Mr. Blood. "Tell us the story."

"Well, it's a sad tale," said Tom. "Three years ago, the same ship came here, just like this. We woke up one morning, and there it was. The harbor master then was a man called Pete. He rowed out to the ship, and he went on board to take a look around."

Old Tom went on. "Pete went below deck, and we heard him shout. Before we knew what was going on, the anchor came up and the ship headed out to sea by itself.

"Some of us got in a boat and chased after it, but it was too fast. I don't know how a ship with no crew could sail out to sea. But that's what we saw."

Old Tom paused and looked out to sea. "We always wondered what happened to poor old Pete. We never saw or heard of him again. But none of us wanted to see that ship come back. We called it the Ghost Ship.

"And now it has returned. So we need your help, Mr. Blood," said Tom.

Chapter 2

On Deck

Old Tom rowed them out into the harbor in a small boat.

"Do we *all* need to go on the ship?" Edgar moaned. He felt ill. His face was a strange shade of green.

"You're not going to be sick, are you?" teased Mary.

Edgar just groaned and stared ahead.

When they were close enough to the ship, Tom stopped rowing. They all stared up at the ghost ship.

The black paint on the side was cracked and peeling.

"Ahoy there!" called Tom. "Is anyone aboard? Are you there, Pete?"

There was only silence.

"Well then," said Mr. Blood. "Let's go and have a look."

Tom threw a rope ladder with hooks up onto the ship's deck. He tugged at the ladder, and it stayed in place. They all climbed up.

In a few moments, the four of them stood aboard the ghost ship.

Up close, the ship still seemed lifeless. Everything metal was covered in rust. The deck was caked in salt. The torn sails flapped limply.

"There's nothing to see here," said Mr. Blood. "We'd better go and look down below."

Mr. Blood strode across the deck to the main hatch. He opened it and climbed down inside the ship.

Chapter 3

Inside the Ship

Edgar and Mary could hear Mr. Blood moving around below deck, opening and shutting things.

Then he called up to them.

"Get down here," he shouted. "And bring something we can use to break down a door."

Edgar looked around the deck and saw a small ax. Its blade was rusty, but it was all he could find. He picked it up.

Mary and Tom had already gone down the hatch.

Mr. Blood was looking at a closed door near the front of the ship.

"I had a quick look around," he said. "There is no one here. Then I found this door. It's locked and I can't find a key. I want to break it open."

Edgar handed the ax to Mr. Blood. "But are you sure we should open the door?" he asked. "If this is such a bad ship, can't we just sink it?"

"I want to find out what happened to Pete," said Tom.

Edgar sighed. He didn't like danger. Mary smiled. She loved it!

"Right," said Mr. Blood. "Let's have a look." He got ready to hit the door.

But just as he was about to bring the ax smashing down, the door swung open by itself.

Mr. Blood's eyes opened wide at what he saw inside the room.

Old Tom put a hand to his mouth.

Mary gasped.

Edgar turned green again.

The room was filled with a huge pile of human bones.

Chapter 4

Trapped!

Mr. Blood bent down and put the ax on the floor.

"Stay here," he said to the others. They didn't argue with him. Mr. Blood took a deep breath and stepped into the room.

As soon as he was in the room, the door slammed shut.

Edgar and Mary shouted in terror.
Mr. Blood began banging on the door.

"I can't open the door!" Mr. Blood
shouted.

Tom and Edgar pulled at the door.
It didn't open.

Then they heard a loud clanking,
rattling sound from above. It sounded as
if the anchor was being raised.

Slowly, the ship was beginning to move. It wasn't just rocking in the water. It had started turning around.

"I remember this happened when Pete went aboard three years ago. The anchor came up, and the ship sailed away," said Tom.

"But who is pulling it up?" cried Mary. "We must stop them!"

"Let's go up and look," said Edgar. He picked up the ax and gave it to Tom.

"Tom, break down the door," Edgar said. "Get Mr. Blood out."

Tom started to hit the door with the ax.

Edgar and Mary ran back up to the deck.

Up in the open air, it seemed as if the ship had come alive. The anchor lay on the deck. The ropes were coiled up. The sails were stretched out from the masts.

"But there is still nobody here!" shouted Mary.

"The ship must be haunted," said Edgar. "All those bones . . ."

Mr. Blood and Tom came up on deck. Old Tom had let Mr. Blood out of the room.

"It's not haunted by their ghosts, my boy," Mr. Blood said. "Those poor people were trapped in there by the ship itself."

"One of them was Pete," added Tom. "Look, this was his hat."

"So what's going on?" asked Edgar.

"It's the ship doing all this," said Mr. Blood. "Don't you see? The ship kills anyone who comes aboard. Now it is trying to kill us."

"Then there's only one thing to be done," said Mary. "We'll have to kill the ship."

Chapter 5

Kill the Ship!

"What do we do?" asked Edgar. "Can we smash a hole in the ship's bottom with the ax?"

"Not a chance," said Tom. "The sides are too thick."

"So how can we kill a ship?" Mary asked.

"The only way to stop the ship is to sail her onto the rocks and leave her there to sink," said Tom. "I can do that."

"Look out!" shouted Mary.

A heavy metal hook on a rope was swinging down from the rigging. It hit Tom's leg.

He cried out and fell to the deck, holding his knee. He tried to stand and fell down again.

"My leg is broken," he cried. "You'll have to try to steer the ship to the rocks. I'll tell you what to do . . ."

Old Tom shouted out orders. Mr. Blood stood at the wheel and steered the ship.

Edgar and Mary ran around the deck, pulling on the ropes that set the sails.

The ship was pointing toward the mouth of the harbor and out to sea. Outside the harbor mouth they could see a line of jagged rocks.

All the time, the ship kept trying to hurt them.

Edgar ducked as another hook skimmed over his head. As he crouched down, he saw the ax lying on the deck.

Of course! he thought. *I can just cut the sails loose, and then the ship won't be able to move.*

He ran over to the mast and started hacking at the ropes that held the sails up.

The ship lurched to one side. The wheel spun.

The wheel hit one of Mr. Blood's hands with a cracking sound. He gasped in pain and stepped back.

Edgar turned just in time to see one of the huge booms swinging across the deck toward him. He had no time to get out of the way.

The boom pushed Edgar across the deck.

As he reached the edge of the ship, one of the ropes on the floor coiled itself around his leg.

He tripped over and fell against the ship's rail. The rail gave way, and Edgar plunged into the water.

Edgar hated boats, but he was a very good swimmer.

He swam away from the boat and then treaded water. When he looked up, the boat was sailing away from him.

"Swim for the rocks!" yelled Mr. Blood. His voice already sounded a long way off.

Edgar could see that Mary was at the wheel and was trying to turn it.

But it was too strong for Mr. Blood, thought Edgar. *What chance does Mary have?*

Chapter 6

Swim for Your Life!

Edgar looked around. He was outside the harbor. The closest land was the jagged rocks he had seen earlier. They looked a long way away.

He started to swim to the rocks.

He hoped that Mary would be able to turn the ship around. The tide was pulling him toward the rocks, and soon he found he had swum halfway there.

He treaded water for a few moments, looking back to see where the ship was. He could see it in the distance.

It was turning around!

But as he looked harder, his heart sank. Mary was not at the wheel. Nobody was. And that meant that the ship was turning *itself* around.

In a few seconds the ship was pointing right at Edgar. It began to cross the waves, coming toward him.

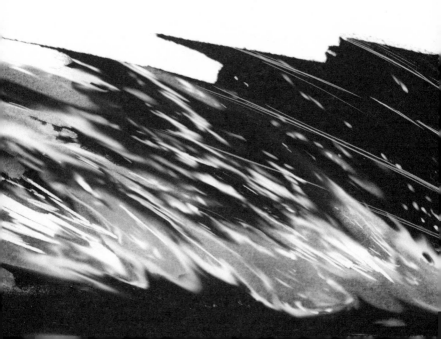

It's coming to get me! Edgar thought. He was very scared.

Edgar kicked his feet hard and swam toward the rocks as fast as he could. But he was getting tired, so he was moving more slowly.

He looked over his shoulder and saw that the ship was racing through the water, helped along by the tide.

He kicked again. This time, one of his feet hit something hard.

"Rocks!" shouted Edgar.

He looked down through the water and saw that he was swimming above a huge, sharp flake of rock.

Edgar followed the ridge of the rock with his feet. It was just under the surface of the water. Then it started dipping away again.

He swam as fast as he could. He had to reach the rocks before the ship got him.

Edgar looked back and saw that the ghost ship was close behind him. The ship seemed to loom over him. It looked huge.

Edgar knew it would hit him in a few seconds. He saw Mary leaning over the side of the ship. She was waving and shouting at him to get out of the way.

At least she's still alive, he thought as he closed his eyes.

The next thing he heard was an ear-splitting, scraping, screeching crunch.

The ship screamed as it hit the hidden rocks and was cut open. It tipped over to one side. Mr. Blood, Mary, and Tom all fell into the water.

"The rocks!" yelled Edgar. "Swim for those rocks! Get away from the ship!"

The four of them swam for their lives. Edgar helped pull Tom along, and Mary helped Mr. Blood.

At last they scrambled onto the rocks. A loud crack like a cannon shot made them all jump and turn.

The ghost ship had snapped in two. With a final groan, it sank beneath the waves.

"Well done, Edgar," said Mr. Blood. "We could not sail the ship. But when you swam to the rocks, the ship came after you. You were very brave."

"And look!" said Mary. "A boat is coming from the harbor to pick us up."

"Oh, no," groaned Edgar. "Not another boat!"